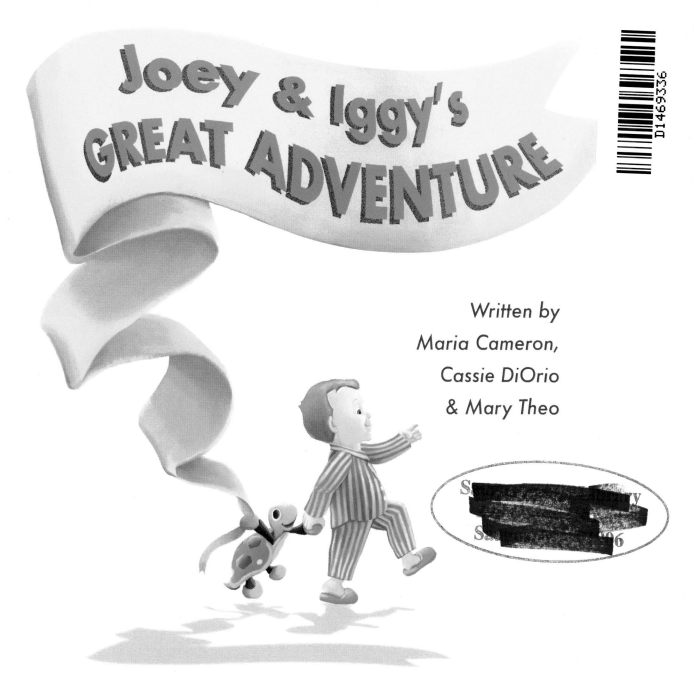

Joey & Iggy's GREAT ADVENTURE

Written by
Maria Cameron,
Cassie DiOrio
& Mary Theo

Illustrated by Erica Leigh & Edited by Speros Zakas

To my son: You are so special and you shine a light wherever you go.
I love seeing the world through your eyes.
Dada and I are so honored to be your parents. You are our hero.
We love you so much, little one.
Love, Mama

Joey's cheeks are as plump as grapefruits;

his kisses are soft, but his hugs are tight.

When Joey is not feeling well,

he holds his pet turtle Iggy with all of his might.

Like Iggy's hard, round shell,
Joey is unbreakable.

Any tough tasks he is given,
he proves he is capable.

Joey is under the weather today.

He wishes he could be outside, having fun.

He hugs his Mommy tight, and she says,

"Lie down and get some sleep;
I love you, little one."

She closes the curtains
and blows him a kiss.

"When you wake up,
you will be at your best.
You have had a long day, my love.
It is time to get some rest."

Joey's Mommy leaves the room
and as she closes the door,
he whispers to Iggy,

Joey is ready to have some adventures
with his favorite turtle along for the ride.

He closes his eyes and begins to imagine
the fun he can have with Iggy by his side.

"We can ride in a rocket ship high in the sky
or explore a castle in a faraway land.
We can go to the park and then swim at the beach,
to ride out the waves and put our toes in the sand!"

"Let's go to a fancy party
and drink from a chocolate fountain.
Then, put on our hiking boots
and climb to the top of the highest mountain!"

Joey puts on his helmet and signals to Iggy
to hop on his bike and prepare for the trip.

They ride through the city, over bumps and some puddles,
as Joey is strong, never losing his grip.

Although Joey is tired, he is not ready to rest.
He wants to make one more stop with his friend.
The wide-brimmed hat comes out of his toy chest,
and one last journey must happen before day's end.

Joey and Iggy see a lion snoozing in the scrub
and are happy to see a Mommy rhino and her calf.
As they walk through the brush, they cross a wildebeest
and then while looking up, spot a newborn giraffe!

Their safari adventure is thrilling and wild,
as Joey cruises with Iggy in a safari jeep.
He turns the wheel and steps on the brakes,
and is now ready to get into bed and fall asleep.

Joey takes four giant elephant steps toward his bed
and climbs under the covers with Iggy in tow.
He looks at Iggy with heavy and happy eyes and says,

"Iggy, you mean more to me than you'll ever know."

For Iggy has been with Joey since he was a tot,
and remains as a reminder that he will be okay.
They go on wondrous adventures together
when Joey cannot be with friends and play.

As Joey drifts off to sleep with Iggy on his pillow,
his Mommy checks in to say goodnight to the two.

Joey smiles when his Mommy kisses his forehead,
as he looks back on his day with his best turtle friend.
The day started off sour, but the two made it better,
for he and Iggy are best buds who can play pretend.

About the Authors & Illustrator

Maria Cameron: Maria enjoyed writing this book about her nephew Joey. She lives in a suburb in Massachusetts with her husband Rob, daughter Olivia, and son Ashton. Maria is a Special Education/English Language Arts Teacher.

Cassie DiOrio: Cassie loved being able to contribute her ideas for this book about her son. She hopes this book will bring joy to children everywhere. Cassie lives in a suburb in Massachusetts with her husband Joe, her son Joey, and his pal Iggy.

Mary Theo: Mary was thrilled to collaborate with her daughters and Erica on this book about her grandson Joey. She lives in a suburb in Massachusetts with her husband John. Mary works full time as the Alliance Talent Leader at RSM US LLP.

Erica Leigh: Erica enjoys working in a variety of mediums, including digital illustration as well as acrylic and watercolor portraits. Having worked with children throughout her career, Erica found this project to be especially meaningful!
www.ericaleighart.com

Made in the USA
Middletown, DE
06 July 2019